Dedicated to my wife Lin(and support this book wou lished for many different r year that has been like no ot ... march 2020 I had a cyst removed from my brain which left me with a visual impairment. I came out of hospital just as the world was changing in a way that impacted everyone's life. Linda put me back on my feet and kept me safe. As part of my recovery I began writing short stories.

This is my first venture into the world of publishing. I hope you enjoy it.

Thank you Linda. You saved me....

21 SHORT TALES WITH A TWIST

Contents

All characters are fictional and any resemblance to any persons is purely coincidental.

THE INTERVIEW

I had checked my watch for the umpteenth time in the last few minutes and also thought about changing the shirt that I was wearing. After reading every book in the library on interview techniques and spending many a night trawling through web pages on the subject, I had opted for a plain blue shirt, no tie, and smart pants. Although the web forums seemed undecided on whether a tie was necessary these days, I had decided to keep it casual and let my mouth and body language do the talking.

I arrived at the interview five minutes early and knocked firmly on the door, hoping the knock didn't sound too forceful. God! I was nervous and overthinking everything.

The door opened and a woman greeted me with a welcoming smile that eased my nerves just a little.

"Please come in and take a seat," She said in a soft calm manner.

"And relax." She added.

I sat down on the chair which I noticed was slightly lower than the three interviewers' chairs. A power tactic I remembered from one of the books that I had read.

"My name is Lydia and this is Olivia, head of personnel and Steven entertainments manager." gesturing towards each person in turn as she introduced them. All of the interviewers had notepads and pencils and were already scribbling away on them.

I re-focused and attempted a smile but felt like I had done an impression of the Cheshire cat from Alice In Wonderland, a big dumb grinning impression. Steven muffled a laugh which confirmed my suspicions were right.

"Ok ! Mr. Wright, please can you tell us a little about yourself to get the ball rolling, hobbies, pastimes, etc."

I had rehearsed this many times in my head and so I began.

" I am 27 and I follow our local football team County, I enjoy walking and reading and I love to cook."

"What type of food do you like to cook?" Olivia jumped in "And what would you say is the best meal you can cook?"

"I love to cook all sorts from pies to roasts but my favourite is Italian pizzas, I make the bases from scratch.

I am also good at making healthy shakes from fruit and vegetables. I am engaged to a lovely lady and I have two stepchildren."

"So you have a good knowledge of all cooking, which is of course very handy given the job you are applying for." Remarked Steven.

"Yes I would say I do, I am quite happy on my own when preparing meals but I am also happy to work as part of a team if the meal is a big one."

A classic answer I thought, but then Olivia threw me

a curve-ball.

I had expected a question along the lines of, if you could be any animal what would you be and why? A classic interview question in order to test you thinking on your feet.

"Tell us a joke and make us laugh." Olivia said as she crossed her arms in expectation.

I racked my brain and looked at each of the interviewers in turn biding me a few precious seconds.

I straightened myself up

"What do you call bears with no ears ?"

They all looked at each other and shrugged

" We don't' know what do you call bears with no ears," The woman asked

"B." I replied.

There was silence and then laughter, from all three of them. Back of the net, I thought.

I was asked several more standard questions including why I thought I was suitable, strengths, weaknesses, etc. Which I answered fairly confidentlly.

The interview ended and I was asked to wait outside and they would ask me to come back in, in a few minutes, once a decision had been made.

I thanked them all and left. Once outside the room, I couldn't help myself and put my ear to the door hoping I could pick up a few words as they talked about me.

I completely lost track of time and before I knew it I found myself falling into the room as the door was quickly opened by Olivia. Overbalancing I did a little forward roll on the floor and managed to get to my feet just before I hit my head on the table.

I peered over the top of the table and saw Steven and Lydia laughing.

"Get up you clown you will be please to know that we think you will be a brilliant daddy and yes you can marry mummy.

Both kids ran to me and attached themselves to my legs.

"Now what were you saying about pizza" Steven chirped up. Lydia took my hand and squeezed it as she kissed me softly

"How did you find that," she asked.

Toughest interview of my life I replied.

The Great British Fake Off

"What time you starting work in Marge's garden ?" Sheila asked her husband Fred.
"I'm setting off in about 10 minutes and will be back about 4pm."Fred replied
Fred was Marge Donnelly's gardener and he did 3 days a week. Her garden was a lot bigger than the average garden in the village and covered almost one and a half acres.
Fred climbed into his van and sounded his horn as he pulled away from his house.
Sheila had planned to spend the day baking, as no doubt she thought her friend Marge Donnelly would be, as the village fair and baking competition was only three weeks away. Sheila although good friends with Marge was very frustrated and Jealous that Marge had won 1st place for the past three years in the best cake competition. Despite Sheila practicing daily, she had failed to create the perfect recipe that would give her victory. However that morning Shelia had a plan that may just swing it for her this year.
As usual, Fred arrived back at 4pm and placed a large piece of cake carefully wrapped onto the kitchen table. "From Marge," Fred whispered as he knew another perfect slice of cake would be like rubbing salt into the wound.

"Busy day, Fred ?" Sheila asked

"Very, managed to clear all the brambles from near the stream ."

"Are you having a cup of tea with that cake ?"

"No cake for me thanks, I had some at Marge's."

The same process was repeated for the next two weeks, Fred arriving home with a slice of perfect cake from Marge, but he did not eat the cake, so Sheila carefully placed the slices of cake into airtight Tupperware boxes and hid them away in a dark cupboard in the pantry without Fred Knowing.

Sheilas devious plan she thought was pure genius.. One day whilst Fred was out at work Sheila took out all the slices of cake she had been saving and placed them together forming a perfect full circle and a complete cake. To disguise the cake she covered it in chocolate ganache and decorated the top with lines of white icing. Sheila stood back from the cake and was convinced that this cakeeven though it was baked by baked by Marge was the cake to beat Marge in the competion. Fight fire with fire Sheila thought. When Fred returned from work that afternoon he too was impressed by the cake that lay before him.

"The proof my dear will truly be in the pudding well the taste will be anyway."

The day of the village fair arrived and the baking competition. All the cakes were placed on the tables in the large marquee. Each cake had been allocated a number so the bakers identities remained completely anonymous. Sheila was number 7 which she was delighted at, as it was her lucky number and Marge was number 13 which made Sheila even happier.

Fred had accompanied his wife to the marquee completely unaware of what his wife was up-to.

The judges took their time going from one cake to the next, marking them on appearance, difficulty of construction, and of course, most importantly taste. The tent became quiet as the head judge Major Watson raised his hand in the air and asked for silence.

He thanked all the entrants and proclaimed the standard got better and better each year. Sheila was bursting with anticipation.

"In second place this year with a beautiful jam sponge is number 13, can that person please come forward."

A small gasp swept around the marquee as Marge the winner of the last three years stepped forward to claim her second-place trophy.

Sheila was ecstatic, Marge second. Sheila bit her bottom lip and squeezed her number 7 card

The major continued.

"And this year the winner of the village bake-off is.......number..5."

Stepping forward with his number to receive the first prize was Fred

"What's going on Sheila blurted out?"

"I have been having baking lessons," Fred exclaimed, "For the sole purpose of putting an end to this rivalry between you two good friends." Nodding towards both his wife and Marge.

"Anyone fancy a cup of tea with a slice of cake?" Fred said, "You can both try mine."
They all tucked in.
"Delicious !" They all said in unison.
What Fred never told his wife was who had been giving him his baking lessons. Marge gave Fred a wink as they enjoyed their cake.

Piece and Quiet

The kettle's steam rose into the air, an expectant mug containing coffee granules sat beside it on the kitchen top. Outside of the window, a perfectly mown lawn invited a chequered blanket to be spread on it which was being held by the lady who had long grey hair. Two children doing handstands, dirty knees and big smiles were just visible in the corner. The blooming red and white roses looked beautiful and the spray of next door's garden sprinkler created a faint rainbow overhead, The garden sheds recently treated door just lovingly painted by an enthusiastic gardener with no legs. But soon he would have legs. Then he would be complete. The last piece of my jigsaw was slotted into place. I went into the kitchen and flicked the kettle back on again. I looked out of the window the lawn looks good I thought. Although I loved the photo jigsaw of my mother in the garden with the children, it did make me sad as it was one of the last photos of my mother to be taken before she passed away. It was a lovely thought of Jeff to have turned the photo into a jigsaw puzzle

Jeff my husband waved from the shed so I reciprocated and held up my mug signalling it was coffee time. As he came into the house he noticed the jigsaw. "Still one piece to go eh?"

You looked puzzled " he added laughing

"I just finished it stop teasing." I walked over to the jigsaw and there was indeed a piece missing. "That's where the chequered blanket is in the picture, that's odd, I thought I had put all the pieces down."Just then both kids came running into the house "Mum, Grandma said she wants her blanket back."

I dropped my coffee.

BOOKMARK

Not long now Harry thought. 21 pages in fact. But his eyes were tired and no matter how much he fought it, he had to give in. He carefully inserted his bookmark and gently placed the book on his bedside unit.

"What sort of rubbish are you reading now Harry ?" Harry's wife on the other side of the bed snapped.

"How to be happy with what you've got," Harry replied

 "What a load of rubbish, if you ask me, just like the book you read before that. What was it ? Living the dream, or living your life, whatever it was, what a load of tosh."

"Yes dear." Harry whispered. Harry fell asleep almost instantly and only woke when his wife yanked back the curtains and let the early morning light stream in.

"I need running into town this morning and while we are out I need you to call and collect my friend Brenda from bridge club and take her to the chiropodist for 1pm."

"Yes, dear." That night Harry finished his book and the following morning was up bright and early much to the annoyance of his wife who always liked to start the day by waking him up by yanking the curtains back. "I am out all day at Joan's, so it would be a good time for you to paint the back room. "Harry had no intention of painting anything.

Harry would have loved to see his wife's face when she arrived home, but then again maybe not. At 5pm the front door opened and in strode Harrys' wife. She looked puzzled, as on the kitchen table lay a wrapped present with a bow, with a card that read, for my wife, enjoy Harry. She ripped open the present and out dropped a book, in fact, the book that Harry had just finished "How to be happy with what you've got" She flicked through it and out fell a piece of paper, Harrys' bookmark. It was a photocopy of a lottery ticket from 6 months ago about the time she thought that Harry had started reading stupid titled books. Out of curiosity, she checked the numbers on the lottery website and much to her shock saw that that week one winner had scooped 3.4 million. The numbers matched. She sat down at the table and started to read, in fact, she didn't stop until she had read it all.

Harry was also reading many miles away, not a book but instructions on how to operate the air conditioning on his yacht.

POST IT NOTES

Mike loved using post-it notes. In fact, Mikes' life revolved around them. Everything he did, every list, every job there was a post-it note. On the fridge "Get Eggs," in the fridge "Milk," on phone "Ring Stuart reg game," on the tv "adjust Arial." The post-it notes went on and on and on. He stared at his last post-it note he'd written "Date 21st Thursday Sarah 7.30 pm." He wrote another "get a new shirt before Thursday." Mike was certain that she could be the girl for him, working in accounts she was smart, not too smart though, not smarter than him. She was a looker and she had only just joined the firm. No one really knew much about her. Only that she had moved from down south and she was renting a flat on the docks. A very nice flat if the rumours were to be true. They'd met at the photocopier and he'd noticed a post-it note stuck to her backside. It read Yoga wed 7pm.   "Off to yoga Wednesday Sarah?" He'd quipped. "How do you know that?" She'd replied full of suspicion. He plucked off her the post-it note stuck to her backside and handed it to her. She relaxed and smiled They had spent the rest of the week flirting and leaving post-it notes around the office. Sarah had an air of mystery about her that Mike was determined to crack. She was not on Facebook, didn't have a Twitter account, and she never mentioned her past life down south. He had to be careful though because he'd felt on a couple of occasions he'd been a bit pushy and she clammed up. Thursday came 7.25pm, he rang her doorbell. No answer so he rang again. Nothing. Bit odd he thought. So mike being mike wrote a post-it note and popped it through the letterbox. Then curiosity got the better of him and he knelt and peered through the letterbox. He saw a small hall and at the end a kitchen with the fridge covered in post-it notes. He smiled and then froze as right in the middle of all the other post-it notes was a post-it note that read KILL MIKE. Mike stood up, surely he wasn't that irritating with his questions about her past. Then his phone rang it was Sarah. He cut the call and ran, ran fast, ran all the way to the police station.

Sarah sat on the bed mopping Katy's brow. "Thanks for popping over Sarah." Katy's mum said "This interview is really important. I am sure Katy's fever

will subside soon."
" I left a post-it note on my fridge reminding me K ill ring mike but I rushed out and didn't see it, I bet he is waiting for me now". Sarah replied worryingly

"So let's get this straight," The detective said "You had a date with a woman called Sarah and she left a post-it note on her fridge to reminder her to kill you?"

I only told you to blow the bloody doors

Genie walked into the kitchen flicked the kettle on

and removed one mug from the mug tree. Tossing a tea bag into the mug like a marksman she sat at the table and waited for the kettle to finish boiling. On the table lay a glasses case, Normans glasses case and she suddenly felt the tears welling up inside her. She removed the glasses and instinctively unfolded them checked for smudges and began cleaning them. She tutted "He never kept them clean." She didn't even know why she was cleaning them, Norman would no longer be wearing them, he would no longer do his Michael Caine impression from The Italian job that made her laugh so much. That impression was what drew her to him at a dinner party held by some friends. Everyone was taking it in turns to do a party piece and when Norman did his Michael Caine it had everyone in stitches including Genie. They ended up chatting the remainder of the night and the rest they say is history. Genie pulled herself together and placed the glasses back in their case. She would never throw them away, so put them in one of the kitchens draws just as the kettle clicked and boiled, Just then Norman walked in and startled Genie "Have you been crying, love?" "Oh it's just me being silly, I miss your Michael Caine

impression, it never fails to make me smile."
"Well, that's good then, as I picked these up from town. Norman put some fake glasses on with plain glass in them and said "I only told you to blow the bloody doors."' Genie started laughing her head off and then gave Norman a big hug and kiss. "I didn't

think I would get to see that again since you had eye

laser surgery ."

Fall From Grace

Mike sat looking out of the window, head in his hands although he was just staring into space. He'd had it all, car, houses, money, loads of money but now it was all gone. His fall from grace had been quick. His family had been supportive to an extent, except his sister who he had felt had taken pleasure from his turn of misfortune, She said he'd got too big for his boots and it had served him right. Ironic really he thought given that he'd lent her money on a couple of occasions and bailed her out when she couldn't make the rent. She still snidely said, "The bigger they are the harder they fall."

By God had he fallen. Not a penny to his name. When things had been good they had been really good. His car a silver jag and a property in one of the most exclusive locations in the city. His parents had tried to console him, but Mike was not listening. The rage swelled inside him and his parent's voices became a blurry annoying drone, he couldn't stand it any longer and stood up and screamed startling his sister. He lunged forward and picked up the board sending it flying into the air. "Mikey !" Mum said in a disapproving manner "It's only a game." Mike began to cry and stomped off to his room. Mike's sister taunted him "Loser, loser." The door to Mike's bedroom slammed shut. The monopoly board and its pieces were strewn across the floor. The silver jag lay on its side.

THIS TIME ITS WAR

The shots whooshed over their heads, but they kept low to the ground out of sight. The machine gun sounds continued for a couple of minutes, then there was shouting but Greg couldn't make out the words. "Stay low, stay low."Greg ordered his men "On my say move to the left behind that big mound and we will try and see where they are. "1,2,3, go." They crawled on their hand and knees for several metres and suddenly stopped in their tracks as Johnny let out a cry as he knelt on something sharp. They carried on a little further and the shouting although louder was still muffled due to all the surrounding noises. Johnny shouted "Incoming." as a bomb exploded nearby, but fortunately, no one was near enough to suffer any impact. The shouting came again but now it was clear "Boys come out dinners ready". Johnny stood up and was caught full in the face with a water bomb. The boys fell about laughing as they discarded their water pistols and squirt guns and then ran towards the house where Greg's' mum was stood holding a huge plate of hot dogs and chips.

The Greatest mystery tour of all

"Name please. "The guide asked, his clipboard and a pen, poised ready to tick the appropriate box.

"Felicity Mayflower."

"Thank you, please take a seat on the right-hand side of the coach."

Felicity made her way along the aisle and found that the only seat available was next to a gentleman near the back. "Excuse me do you mind if I sit here ? I have been asked to sit on the right-hand side and this is the last seat."

"Why of course not, would you prefer the window seat?" Replied the man who stood up in expectation.

"The aisle seat is fine thank you." Felicity responded. Felicity settled into her seat and the gentleman offered his hand accompanied by a warm smile and introduced himself. "Roger, pleased to meet you." Felicity and Roger chatted away from the moment they met and did not even notice the coach pulling out of the bay and heading off on their mystery tour. The tannoy squealed as the guide adjusted the volume and tapped the microphone. "Good morning all." Announced the guide

"Good morning." at least half of the people on the coach responded

 "Thank you for joining us this morning and what a lovely morning it is." The guide added. "I would like to take this opportunity to introduce myself. My name is Peter and I shall be your guide on the first half of this journey. The second half will be lead by Ike." Ike stood up and halfheartedly waved "The first leg of our journey today will take approximately one and a half hours, so sit back and enjoy the ride and the views and I will inform you when we are about 10 minutes away from stopping."

"One and a half hours away." The man across the aisle from Felicity said grumpily and loud enough for most of the people on the coach to hear

"My legs won't last that long without a good stretch, Peter, any chance of swapping seats with that chap near the front, he has got loads of legroom?"

"I can ask sir if he would mind swapping, won't be a moment." Peter returned moments later and informed him that he had asked but the reply was a no. Felicity leaned over close to Roger and whispered

"Is that the man who was in the local paper campaigning for the reinstatement of free tea and coffee in the library on Wednesdays.?" Roger glanced over and nodded

"Affirmative." Roger added

The campaigner continued to moan for the next few minutes until eventually when he realized that no one was listening suddenly fell asleep.

Felicity and Roger laughed quietly and continued chatting about everything and nothing and only stopped briefly as Peter worked his way down the aisle and handed them a cup of complimentary tea and a biscuit. How lovely they agreed we didn't expect that.

"Always expect the unexpected."Peter said as he winked.

"Did you see that crime drama last night on BBC1?" Roger asked hoping she had

"Oh yes I did and wasn't it great, such a twist at the end and to think it was based on a true story. Did they really think they would get away with it ?"

"Load of rubbish it was, what a waste of two hours of my life." The campaigner chirped up now awake

"Not everyone's cup of tea I know," Roger said trying to make light of the campaigners cutting comment

"But not as good as this cup of tea." Roger quipped raising his plastic cup in a cheers salute in the direction of the campaigner. Felicity could not help but roar with laughter. It was a good ten minutes before the campaigner had stopped moaning about missing out on his free cup of tea and biscuit and that he expected a small refund at some point. "Any idea yet where we are going?" asked Roger

"No idea at all but the weather is turning, have you seen the mist?" Roger looked out of the window and could see mist swirling around "It's quite thick in places too," He said "Would you like to explore where we are going to.... " Roger had not even finished his sentence and Felicity had said yes. "So that's settled then the unknown awaits and we shall explore it together". Once more the tannoy squealed and Peter's voice filled the air. "This is your ten-minute notice, we shall be arriving shortly, please listen carefully to the following instructions." "Ooooh !" Roger whispered to Felicity, sounds intriguing   "All those sat on the right side of the coach looking forwards," Peter gestured pointing to his left "Shall be disembarking first, this is due to the space available at our destination. All those on the left-hand side please remain seated until further instruction."

"Bloody marvellous." The campaigner grumbled " Just my luck, last off as always."

By now the coach had slowed down to almost a crawl as the mist had increased and visibility was only about ten metres.

The coach then stopped and Peter once more took to the tannoy. "Right-hand side only please."

Felicity and Roger stood up and made their way back up the aisle and got off the coach. Once all the people on the right-hand side of the coach were off Peter said follow me and held up a bright torch that was almost blinding if you looked directly at it.

Everyone shuffled along and Felicity reached for Roger's hand and he reciprocated and held hers tight.

They arrived at some big gates where Peter produced his clipboard and once more ticked off those present.

"Straight through and straight-ahead" Peter calmly said.

"Where are we" Felicity asked, Peter.

Peter placed his hand on her and Roger's shoulders and smiled warmly.

Back on the bus the campaigner stood up and snapped "How long we going to be kept on this coach, it has been ages, and can you do something with the air con it's too hot on here?"

"Sit down and be quiet" Ike snapped back.

"Where you're going mate its gonna get a lot hotter."
Ike added

Ike flicked a switch and the coach door slid shut.
"Buckle up people" and Ike hit the pedal and the
coach sped off into the mist. Ike's cap fell off as he
took the first corner at great speed revealing his little horns.

DON'T CALL ME STEVIE

My head throbs like I have never known. It's all I feel. I tell a lie, I feel, I feel like my body is not mine. I ache, my whole body aches.

"Morning sleepy." A voice enters my brain. I cannot process the voice because I do not recognize it. I think hard, where am I? I open one eye and the streaming light through the window shocks me, it feels like a laser. I quickly shut it to relieve the pain.

"How do you like your bacon?" The voice again. Bacon, did they say bacon? It was a female voice. I am lead down and can feel the warmth of the covers that surround me. I open my eyes carefully once more and as the room comes into focus I feel a rush of panic as I do not recognize it. I wait a while for my brain to catch up and then piece together items, objects, and layout of the room so that I will suddenly remember where I am, But I don't. My memory has failed me. I sit bolt upright and stare at the person who has been speaking. I do not know them. "Eggs, scrambled, fried, or poached"? The girl is standing at the cooker in a long shirt. She has shoulder length blonde hair. She looks over at me and blows me a kiss. "Where am I and who are you?" I say

" I shall pretend you are joking but ...Stevie, you are in my flat and I am the love of your life"

"Don't call me Stevie, I hate that name it's Steve." I snap back

I feel I am going to throw up and my head starts to spin

I cannot comprehend what is happening. I try to re-boot my brain and remember, but all I get are flashes of memories. I then it hits me. I was on my stag do. I am on my stag do. Did she say the love of my life? This cannot be happening. I am engaged to be married...next Saturday. I love my fianceé, She is an angel, my best friend, she makes me laugh, she is sexy, hot, and I love her, oh god I love her.

I jump up out of bed and shout.

"I don't know who you are and I don't know what I am doing here."

"Well, Stevie let me remind you, do you remember your mates dragging you to The Black Bull?Well, I work at the Black Bull behind the bar and when you walked in with your drunken mates I asked you all to wind it in a bit as you were all a bit lively."

I searched my memory for this fact and yes I did remember a Black Bull pub

The girl continued "Well I managed to calm everyone down and after a while, we got chatting. You told me about how wonderful your wife to be was, that she was hot like you just said and that she was smart and sharp and was also your best friend. You also told me I had lovely eyes and a little bit more besides. In fact, you said I could be a model. My brain did not compute any of this. "Well I was knocking off at 11pm so you offered to walk me home. Jeff your best man, by this stage was semi-conscious as was most of your group, but you had almost sobered up, so you said sure I will walk you home, and then when I asked you in for coffee you couldn't keep your hands off me. Hey, presto here we are Stevie boy". "Stop calling me Stevie, my name is Steve". I shouted again.

My mouth was dry and all I could think about was getting home to my fiancée. I was now aware that I was only stood in my boxer shorts and so scanned the room and saw my pants and my shirt laying on the floor. I walked towards them and felt myself falling face first. I am sure I heard laughter. I hit the deck hard as I now lay face down on the floor.

I jumped up and hurriedly pulled on my pants and threw on my shirt.

"I have to go, this is a mistake I cannot remember any of this."

"But Stevie, we have so much to talk about, plans to make."

"Stop calling me Stevie, no one calls me Stevie." I lunged towards the unknown woman, and then the lights went out just as I..... Then out of nowhere a rumble shook the floor. The bed shook, the cooker, the sink, the whole room began shaking. Either it was an earthquake or this flat was located next to a railway line. The wall in front of me then split into two and slid away from each other. I fell back on the bed in total disbelief. As the walls came apart I could hear the sound of riotous applause and laughter. Bright lights shone in my face and the flat or what was left of it filled with light. A man in a sharp suit stepped into the flat through the gap in the walls. The separated walls now revealed 100s of people in a stand all clapping and laughing hysterically. "What the hell is going on." I shouted but was drowned out by the commotion "Steve Blackledge! you are live on TV please do not swear." I mouthed the words live on TV but nothing came out. The sharp suit man I suddenly recognized. He was the man from the hottest program on TV

" Stevie, Stevie, Stevie." The crowd chanted

"We'd like you to meet someone," The suit guy said in a dramatic voice

Just behind him was Abby my fiance, smiling and laughing accompanied by all the lads from my stag do including Jeff.

The suited man continued "Stevie, thanks for taking part on "Stitch Up", the TV show where reality isn't what it seems and where make-believe becomes reality"

The suit man's face suddenly changed and the confident smile and presence he demanded were substituted by a look of horror. He put his arm up signaling for silence from the audience. He then looked at me straight in the eye and started to back away. His gaze then transferred to the woman who only moments ago was cooking eggs and bacon. She lay on the floor next to the cooker a belt wrapped around her neck. My belt. The girl's eyes were open but she lay motionless. Suddenly one of the crew screamed as the full situation became apparent. She was dead.

"Get an ambulance, get an ambulance and the police."

"He's killed her, during the loss of transmission". Another crew member yelled

My Faiencee screamed too as I said "I didn't mean to do it she kept calling me Stevie."

My cup of tea.

My phone pinged and glancing at the screen the message read "Ok for 9am tomorrow, can I bring Maude with me, my next-door neighbour ? she doesn't get out much and she is fun."

My heart sank as I really wanted to chat to Sue my best mate about my love life, or lack of it. I was going through a bit of a dry spell on the man front and needed a boost and a plan. If anyone could get me back in the game Sue could, but now Maude was coming I guess another few days wouldn't hurt.

"Sure, more the merrier."I replied. At 9am the following day on the dot, my front door bell binged. I opened the door and Sue gave me a great big hug. "Maude changed her mind then?" But before Sue had a chance to reply, out stepped Maude from behind her. Maude must have been under 5ft tall, but was like a whippet and was in my kitchen before I had a chance to welcome her.

"Stick the kettle on then," Maude said as bold as

brass. I obliged and went to retrieve the tea bags from the cupboard. "Use tea leaves, here use these they have a lovely flavour to em." Maude handed me a little bag that also contained a tea strainer. I put my favourite choccy digestives on a plate to accompany the tea, which Maude soon made short work of.

Upfront as she was, there was something about Maude that made me warm to her, and during our half an hour or so chat, found she was a mind of information on every subject we broached.

I picked up the 3 cups to clear away but Maude put her hand on mine and said "Wait!"

My cup was taken away from me and Maude began staring into the bottom of the cup and turning it around three times, then back again three times.

Maude stood up and said

"well I've never seen such a signal as that before, so strong, it's a life changer alright. My lady, you are about to hit the jackpot." I did my very best to hold it together and not laugh, but it eventually it came out and I laughed. Maude commanded Sue to take her home. As I hugged Sue goodbye and thanked her for an interesting morning Sue holding a deadpan expression, whispered in my ear

"Maude is never wrong." Closing the door to be once more consumed by the silence I returned to the kitchen and placed the cups in the dishwasher. The doorbell once more binged and I expected Sue to be stood there having forgotten her bag, coat, or something else ,as she is always prone to leaving items behind. But it was not Sue. It was a man who stood with a microphone and a huge cardboard cheque along with a cameraman filming me. As we stood facing each other, he grinned at me and turning to the camera said "Sheila Bradbury, congratulations you have won our doorstop mystery prize of £10,000, on behalf of Treats dog food, woof woof."

What seemed like minutes passed, but it must have only been only a second or two until I spoke. "Sheila lives across the street at number 26, I am 29 but my number 9 keeps slipping round." The grinning man stopped grinning and the cameraman lowered his camera. Without so much as a sorry, the grinning man turned on his heels and ran across the street to number 26. "You idiot !" shouted the grinning man as he ran "Why didn't you check we had the right house?" The cameraman stepped up to the door where I was stood and said so softly "I am so sorry Mam." He then took my hand and kissed it. He turned towards the grinning man on the other side of the street and shouted.

"Hey Geoff, stick your job, you rude arrogant egomaniac."

Turning back to face me the cameraman smiled and again softly spoken asked

"Do you know where there is a café around here? I have been up since 4am and could murder a coffee."

"I will put the kettle on, come in." I suggested

"And that's how I met your daddy." Sue said as her two children ate their breakfast.

"When is Auntie Maude coming round, she's fun?"

asked the eldest.
I looked into my tea cup
"Soon," I replied, "very soon."

Lot 41 Ticket to ride

The kitchen door flew open and in strode Mike, my husband who plonked a large cardboard box on the kitchen table.

His face was a picture of concentration as he rummaged around inside the box pulling out odds and sods of junk. "Here it is," He proclaimed as he held up a funny-looking object.

"Look at that beauty," he said beaming from ear to ear.

"What is it this time?"I replied halfheartedly.

"This my dear, is a 1917 original WW1 boxed set of field binoculars, it even has an inscription from the owner and underneath it says WW1."

I didn't want to break it to him but I had to. "It can't be original as in 1917 they did not know there was going to be another war so would not have written WW1 on it." Mike paused stared into space for a few seconds and then tossed it back into the box.

"I will be in the shed." He huffed and promptly picked up the box and headed out from where he'd sprung from. During dinner that evening I broached the subject of me spending a night away with some old friends for a catch-up at a spa hotel. Mike was not in a good mood after his dream of fortunes being made from the auctions were once again shattered. "We have not got any spare cash at the moment." Mike informed me."

Although I knew we did have a couple of hundred in the tin for treats mike had firmly pointed out that that was earmarked for buying and selling at the auction. To be honest I didn't see much selling, just buying which dwindled the pot every week. " You could always do a bit of wheeler-dealing your-self Sheila if you think you can do any better." Mike grumpily said.

"Well I might just do that," I snapped back, I sh"all go with you to the auction next Tuesday to view," The week passed and before I knew it Tuesday came along. Mike was up bright and early as he was every Tuesday on auction viewing day. Armed with a little book and a pen, a magnifying glass, and his phone we set off. We spent a good part of the morning rum-maging through boxes and boxes of "stuff" I could see Mike near the corner of the room scratching his head, taking a photo or two, and obviously trying to eavesdrop on two women's conversation. I made my way over to where Mike was and he gestured me to go away in a shooing motion. I glared at him and turned on my heels and went into the café and bought myself a hot chocolate. Several minutes later Mike came into the café all excited. "Sorry, Sheila but you will never guess what I have just heard ?". Mike went on to tell me he had heard two women excitingly talking about a box underneath the counter that contained a black and white photograph. "Big deal". I remarked, "There must be loads of them knocking about like that at auctions". Mike was almost out of breath as he continued. "Well, there are, but one of the women who was talking is I think a specialist in that field as she seemed to know so much about the Beatles and photos."Mike paused and then said even quieter than before. "She said she has never seen that photo before, and she thinks it is unpublished." Mike put his finger to his lips indicating me not to say anything.

"Do you know what that means?"

"Yes ! " I replied, "It means you are probably going to buy another box of junk!"

"There is no probably about it, it could be worth hundreds". Mike didn't even bother to ask me if I had seen anything of interest but insisted we must go home so he could do some research. And research he did, all night into the early hours. Sliding into bed he whispered to me "Are you awake"?

"Yes".I murmured back "Well I can't find it anywhere so tomorrow I will be down the auction early to get a good seat, are you coming?" I had to admire his enthusiasm and as he kissed me goodnight I fell into a lovely deep sleep. Auction day arrived and we found ourselves sitting on the front row a good hour before the auction was due to start. Mike tapped me on the shoulder and nodded in the direction to the right of the auctioneer's stand. It was the two women who he had seen talking about the Beatles photo, The lots rolled by and Mike was fidgeting just like a schoolboy sat at assembly. "Lot 40, a pair of candlesticks ." The auctioneer proclaimed. Mike nudged me with excitement. "Next one, concentrate." He whispered "Lot 41, a box of bric-a-brac, who will start the bidding at £5.00 ?" One of the women's hands went up. The auctioneer acknowledged her."£5.00 on my left,do I see £10.00 ?" Mike's hand went up "£15.00 ?" Again the woman's hand went up. The bidding continued and was soon up to £165.00 I gave Mike a heavy nudge and said "enough."

"I will go to £200.00." He protested   The auctioneer took a mouthful of his coffee and then said "£195.00 to the left of me, do I hear £200.00 ?" Mike put his hand up and once more I gave him a look "£200,00 do I see £205, " The bidding women remained silent and then gave a shake of the head "Going once, going twice.....SOLD." Mike gave a re leaved triumphant fist gesture and turned to me and kissed me. As the auction wound down he paid his money at the cash desk and went to collect his box and smugly asked the two women who were still at the auction to step aside as we wanted to get his box. "Better luck next time ladies," Mike whispered as he left the room. Back at the house mike sat at the table holding his photo in front of him, having discarded the rest of the contents of the box.

"Can I have a look in the box ? "I asked.

"Sure help yourself to anything you want, I have what I wanted. "

I removed a few items and placed them on the table having given them a quick wipe down.

"Didn't we have a vase-like that one"? Mike exclaimed, "And didn't we have a plate similar to that"?

"Yes we did" I replied and this cup and saucer, not forgetting this board game and ..."

Mike looked at me puzzled.

Just then the doorbell rang and I jumped up to answer it.

"Come in ladies, Mike is just admiring his photo and box of items".

Mike looked up and much to his surprise the two women from the auction stood before him.

"What do you two want...this photo is not for sale if that is what you are after"

"Oh no ! one of them said we have just come to give Sheila her earnings from the auction".

A pile of notes was placed on the table along with a receipt.

Sheila counted out the money £170.00 after commission.

Not bad for 1 lot.

Mike's confusion grew as he asked "what lot ?"

"Lot 41." I replied

My two friends sat down at the table as I got up and put the kettle on and one of then said "The thing is mike Sheila mentioned that she did not have enough money to come away with the ladies for a spar week-end and well we thought of a plan to help her raise some funds.The items in the box are yours and the photo...."

"Is worth a few hundred." Mike butted in

"Actually it is fake,"

"Rubbish!" Mike jumped in "How do you know?"

"Because Mike we are all in it, look top left" Mike scanned the photo as he saw his wife and her two friends all waving at him "Did I not mention to Mike that my good friend Karen works in digital media and is a whizz with image creation"? Mike sat in silence for 5 minutes and then suddenly burst out laughing. "Ok, you got me," and placed his hands in the air. "I am off to the shed" As my two friends left they walked outside and could hear singing coming from the shed. "What's that song "? Karen asked. "With a little help from my friends...The Beatles I think ." They laughed all the way home.

The three cavaliers

Huddled close together the three cavaliers kept their heads down against the strong wind and held tightly on to their hats as branches and leaves swirled around them. The coach had dropped them off about ¼ mile away from their destination as word had spread that a couple of trees had come down blocking the only track to the inn. As the cavaliers rounded a corner their hopes were raised as they saw the lights of the Inn twinkling on the hill. There you go fellows one of the cavaliers shouted above the wind as he pointed towards the inn. They drove forward against the wind that seemed to be getting stronger and soon found themselves pushing themselves against the big inn front door. They spilled into the inn taking a swirl of leaves and an icy cold breeze with them. Surprised and slightly annoyed faces greeted them from the people that were already occupying the inn that offered them warmth from the large roaring fire. One man who was sat at the bar turned and shouted "shut that bloody door now, do you want us to freeze to death?"The cavaliers battled with the door and managed to slam it shut just as a couple more drinkers joined in the heckles.

"Sorry good folks," one of the cavaliers said, "The storm is raging out there now."Most of the drinkers were huddled around the fire and the looks the cavaliers received were not that friendly. To try and blend in quickly the cavaliers made their way to the big curved bar that ran the whole length of the Inn. "Three ales when you're ready." A cavalier said. The barmaid spun round

"Three ales what! Manners cost nowt gentlemen."

"Forgive us madam" another replied, "I do apologize." A selection of coins was laid out on the bar the majority of which were removed by the barmaid promptly. The cavaliers lifted their drinks and went off to a spare table just to the left of the fire, near the door. Given the disruption and unfriendly welcome they received, they kept quiet. As they sat down they heard a man tut and curse the disruption to the otherwise Calm ambiance of the inn, "Damn party revelers." one man whispered to his friend. No sooner had the three cavaliers settled at the table, the inn door once more burst open bringing in the accompanying swirl of leaves and an icy cold draft. Stood in the doorway were an astronaut, an alien, and a cowboy." Shut that bloody door," a few of the drinkers shouted in unison. The three new arrivals saw the cavaliers and called out laughing as they approached. "Is it just us here at the moment"? "Right you lot," the barmaid shouted out above the din. "Please can you go through to the room where your office party is at the back you're disrupting the regulars" The astronaut, alien, and cowboy followed by the three cavaliers exited the main inn bar and slipped into a side room where disco lights twinkled.

Hop Skip and a Jump

Kyle Hopkins was running down the school corridor late for his chemistry lesson at 10.30 am. He arrived a few minutes late and his chemistry teacher was not amused unlike the rest of the class that tittered behind hands held to their faces.

"Hopkins! I have had enough of your timekeeping, headmaster's office at 12 noon." The teacher barked

"Yes Sir."Hopkins said bowing his head down in humiliation. At 12 noon on the dot, Hopkins knocked on the headmasters' door and entered. As doing so he nearly fell over a box containing what looked like junk that lay on the floor, along with many other boxes of junk. Hopkins accepted his telling off and promised to improve his timekeeping. The room was stuffy, old fashioned and was dark, shelves of books and old paintings filled the walls, not a very nice place at all thought Hopkins. On his way out back through the corridors, he met Mr. Cartwright the school caretaker who was struggling to carry a huge box and also trying to navigate a door. "Let me get that for you." Hopkins offered. He followed Mr. Cartwright outside and saw him deposit the box in a big yellow skip.

"The headmaster wants his room clearing out today to make way for his new modern furniture that is arriving tomorrow, all ready for the Governor's visit." He told Hopkins.   "I have 45 minutes of free time replied Hopkins let me give you a hand."

Mr. Cartwright who was feeling tired accepted his kind offer, the skip had several boxes and bin bags in it already and it was filling up.

The time seemed to slip away and Hopkins suddenly realized that he only had a few minutes left of his lunch break so headed for the dining hall where he sneakily jumped the queue. Unfortunately, the headmaster was watching and when Hopkins was sat down tucking into his sausage and chips the headmaster sat down opposite him and invited Hopkins to meet with him at 3.30 pm at his office. Hopkins obviously did not have a choice and so accepted his invitation. Once more on the dot Hopkins entered the headmasters' office and took his telling off. Hopkins, however, did not mention why he was late eating and his good deed helping Mr. Cartwright, as he was sure it would get him in trouble. By coincidence, Mr. Cartwright walked in on the telling off having almost cleared the room, and was indeed relieved to hear that Hopkins had kept quiet. Hopkins kept his head down for the next several weeks at school as he knew his report was due and was hoping his two visits to the headmaster would be forgotten.   A few weeks later one Sunday evening the headmaster and his wife were sat in the front room of their home sipping wine and nibbling cheese and biscuits watching the Antiques Road-show on TV. The show had visited a nearby town a few weeks earlier and they both thought it would be interesting to watch. Halfway through the show, a man stood next to the presenter with three paint-ings. Next to the man was a boy of about 15 years old. The headmaster pointed at the screen and said rather loudly " That boy it's BLOODY HOPKINS." "Is that one of your school children then?"The Head-masters' wife replied,

The presenter turned to the man and said "So what can you tell me about these three marvelous paint-ings?" Mr. Hopkins replied, "Well I think they are early 19th century by the artist Hemmings."

"Well let me take a look on the back." flipping one of the paintings over and confirming the painting was indeed by Hemmings and original he then asked, "Where did you acquire them from?"

Mr. Hopkins put his hand on his son's shoulder and proudly said "My son Kyle found them in a skip. The presenter nearly fell over and the crowd that was gathered around gasped in unison.

By now the headmaster was staring at the tv and shouted "They were on my wall in the office the thieving little sod."

The presenter continued

"So I guess you are all wondering if your find is worth much? Well as they are in good condition and are also signed I would put an estimate of between £10,000-£15,000 each." The crowd gasped again as the headmaster spat out his wine.

Kyle jumped up in the air and punched it.

Kyle and his dad high-fived each other as they sat on their sofa along with Kyle's mum and sister as they too were watching the Antiques Roadshow.

Monday morning Kyle arrived at school a little bit earlier than normal, as word had spread about his appearance on TV. Kyle's dad was also present and they both headed for the headmasters' office. They knocked and a short sharp "Enter." Emanated from within. Inside was the headmaster, Mr. Cartwright, and a police officer.

Before the headmaster could speak Mr. Hopkins jumped in

"Headmaster could you please confirm the following. "

"Did you ask your caretaker, Mr. Cartwright, to put those paintings in the skip and to dispose of them? please answer yes or no." The headmaster started mumbling. and then said yes. Turning to Mr. Cartwright Mr. Hopkins asked " Mr. Cartwright did Kyle ask if he could have some of the contents of the skip to recycle as it was going to landfill?"

"YES," Mr. Cartwright replied firmly.

Mr. Hopkins continued, "Therefore as ownership of the paintings has been established by the admission of the Headmaster and Mr. Cartwright I think we are all done, If you have any more questions please call my office and my secretary will book you an appointment."

Mr. Hopkins reached into his suit and pulled out a business card and gave it to the headmaster.

The card read Charles Hopkins, Dealer in Fine art, 175 Station Rd, Erksbridge.

The policeman said, "As all seems to be above board I shall be off." Turned on his heels and left. Mr. Hopkins then added

"My son Kyle asked if he could donate to the school fund for a new minibus as a goodwill gesture to the sum of £5000.00 which I feel is very kind and generous of him." The headmaster was close to tears but fought them back and politely accepted the offer.

Kyle and his dad also left the headmasters office but not before Kyle had commented on what a lovely modern office it now was.

ANOTHER DAY IN PARADISE

Roger stretched his arms out wide and yawned. He stepped out onto the porch and then ran towards the crystal blue waters and shouted to his wife Celia "Just swimming." Not that Celia needed telling, as Roger was a creature of habit and always stretched out and then ran towards the sea for his morning swim. As he had told her many times, he enjoyed an early morning swim before it got too hot and it helped focus his mind for the day ahead. Roger dived into the water and as he did so caught sight of his neighbour Charles waving frantically from the shore. Roger pretended he didn't see or hear him and was soon swimming flat out parallel to the shore. The last thing Roger wanted was Charles moaning about something or nothing. Roger and Charles had known each other for 15 years or more but unfortunately, since the accident, Roger tolerated Charles more than considering him a friend. 30 minutes later Roger stepped from the water and headed back to their home where his wife was waiting with a bowl of fruit and a glass of water.

"Good swim darling ?" Celia asked

"Marvellous, thank you." Roger replied

Celia continued, "Whilst you were out swimming

Jenny and Charles dropped by and have invited us to their place for our evening meal, Charles said he will do his shark steaks on the barby."

"Oh God not again. That's 3 times this week I hope you said no we were busy?"

"Busy! doing what exactly?"

"I don't know, make something up."

We are expected when the sun dips behind the headland.

"Another spectacular sunset with Charles' long-winded philosophical speeches about heaven and paradise and fate blah blah blah."

"Stop being so mean Charles."

Roger stormed off into the trees kicking things as he went. How he longed to be back at work with an inbox bursting at the seams and deadlines, meetings, traffic, noise, people.

But here he was stuck with Charles on this damn tropical island god knows where, Will we ever be rescued he shouted. If it hadn't been for Charles showing off with his new yacht and heading out when the weather reports predicted a storm they wouldn't have ended up stranded on this island. Well, tonight Charles can stick his shark steak where the sun doesn't shine.

It was a pity that Roger spent so much time storming off in the trees or he would have seen the boat on the horizon and sent up their last remaining flare. Oh well, another day in paradise then.

Crash

"OUR RECORDS SHOW YOU HAVE BEEN INVOLVED IN AN ACCIDENT THAT WASN'T YOUR FAULT !"said the voice on the phone.

"Yes I have!" replied Mark rather angrily

The woman seemed surprised "I am sorry to hear that, could you please give me some details, What is your name?"

"James Hunt."

"Mr. Hunt was anyone injured as a result of the accident?"

"Yes, my son Steven was injured."

"Can you please describe the events leading up to the accident?"

"Ok ! this is how I saw it, I was approaching a bend and my son shouted "watch out CAT."

It made me jump, in fact scarred the life out of me, I couldn't break in time, so on the bend the car flipped and landed on its roof"

"Oh My !" The caller responded "And you are telling me YOU were not hurt at all?"

"That is correct."

"You are very lucky sir."

"Not really" Jeff replied I was so angry I clipped my son round the back of the head for making me crash

and he stormed off, just because he was in the lead"
"In the lead, where you racing ?"
"Yes we were racing, my sons scalextric."

Show and tell

Charlie stood by the door waiting patiently for the postman to arrive and hopefully his parcel with it. Charlie loved all things mysterious in-particular all things related to UFOS and he had seen an item on eBay that he just had to have. Using all his saved up pocket money and with the help of his dad, he had bought a piece of alleged alien spaceship wreckage. A knock at the door an hour later and the postman handed Charlie his parcel.

Charlie rushed to the dining table and unwrapped it and when he had he proudly lifted it to the light and stared open-mouthed in awe of his new possession, His dad came in and looked fondly at his son.

"Are you happy with your find Charlie ?"

"Yes dad I am and I know you think it is a waste of money but I have researched this item and it comes from a group of items recovered by UFO watchers in America who said they recovered unusual items from a UFO crash site in the Nevada desert."

Charlie ran his fingers around the item that looked a bit like a cog with a metal plate connected to it and told his dad that he had a show and tell coming up at school and he would like to take the object in to show all his fiends and the rest of the class. Maybe he could persuade others to join the club UFO MINDS UK that he was a member of.

"That would be a good idea ." his dad told him " But don't you think it may be a bit deep and complicated for some of your school friends. What about I help you liven it up a bit and make it fun for everyone.

"What do you have in mind Dad?"
You just leave it to me and plan your talk and I will just make a quick call to run it by your headmaster."
Charlie was very curious but knowing his dad it would be brilliant so off he went to his bedroom to work on his show and tell presentation.
After an hour his mum shouted him for lunch and has he been working so hard he had built up quite an appetite placed his new UFO item on the desk and raced downstairs for his sandwich.
After eating fast and being told off by his mum for doing so Charlie went back upstairs to continue working on his project. He went to his desk but his UFO item was not on there but on the floor. Maybe I knocked it off as a ran for lunch and thought nothing more about it. That night Charlie was woken by what seemed a bright light shining through his window and he got up to take a look thinking that a car's headlights were pointed at his window. But when Charlie got to the window the lights went out.
I bet my dad is playing jokes on me thought Charlie.
The following morning it was the day of the show and tell and Charlie was very excited. He'd also seen his dad putting a bag into the boot of his car without anyone seeing and there seemed to be a silver suit of some sort sticking out but Charlie never said anything.

The teacher thanked Carol for her interesting talk on her trip to Australia and who had made everyone laugh by blowing her didgeridoo. They all clapped as Carol returned to her seat.

"Next we have Charlie who is going to talk to us about his interest in UFOS."

"What's UFOS?" shouted out a boy sat at the back of the class.

Charlie jumped up and said "That is a very good question UFOS are unidentified flying objects."

"Do you mean alien spaceships?" The boy continued.

"Some UFOs may come from outer space, but some may originate from Earth or even from somewhere else like the future for instance. They are like the name suggests unidentified, so no one knows for sure."

Charlie went onto explain that he was a member of a UFO club that searched for answers by looking at all the evidence which included reports, photos, video footage, and also physical evidence.

Charlie lifted out of his bag the alleged UFO wreckage and held it proudly up towards the class.

"This!" Charlie said, is a piece of UFO wreckage that was found in Nevada USA.

"Looks like a bit of old junk to me." One boy said who was sat on the front row.

"Yeah !" Another boy joined in.

Charlie felt he was starting to lose his audience as one or two more boys joined in the heckling.

Mrs. Fairgood the teacher was just about to intervene when the classroom door suddenly burst open and in the doorway stood a figure in silver with a large helmet on its head a bit like a spaceman.

"I come in peace children do not be afraid I am a friendly Alien from far away".

Charlie saw all the faces of the children light up in amazement and excitement as the spaceman walked in between all the desks to the front picked up the piece of UFO wreckage and patted Charlie on the head and saying "Thanks for keeping this safe for us Charlie, we need this to get back home."

The spaceman turned to face the children "Let us keep my visit to ourselves kids, NASA keeps chasing me and I am running out of rocket fuel."

He thanked Mrs fairgood and apologised for the interruption and then strode out of the classroom and was gone.

All the kids cheered and clapped and all agreed that Charlie's show and tell was the best show and tell ever in the history of the world.

Charlie couldn't wait to get home and thank his dad for putting on such a brilliant show and telling him what a great success it had been.

He ran in through the front door and found his dad sat at the kitchen table but he did not look happy.

"What's up dad ? you were brilliant, the class loved the performance."

"What are you talking about Charlie I couldn't make it, I got stuck at work and tried everything to get away but I had an emergency meeting with some clients."

That's impossible a spaceman came to class and took away my piece of UFO wreckage.

Charlie's dad looked genuinely shocked by what

Charlie was saying and listened carefully to Charlie's recollection of the day's events.

The headmaster sat in his office with a slight headache, mostly caused by the noise of the excited children in class 2B and the show and tell incident. He smiled to himself as he walked over to the wardrobe to get his coat, Never a dull moment he thought to himself as he pushed the silver spacesuit to one side and got his coat off the hook. It wasn't every day you got to be an alien at work now was it?

He closed his office door and locked it shut and headed off home for a well-earned glass of wine he was sure his wife had waiting for him. It wasn't until he was well away from the school that the UFO wreckage began to vibrate and fell off his desk onto the floor.

A day at the Zoo

The sun was beating down and David stood starring at the animals basking in the warmth of the rays. He recognised one of the animals and went a little closer to the cage edge to get a better look. He glanced round to see if his mother and father approved of his bravery. They did not react so he took that as a sign it was ok. David waved and he could see a flicker of recognition in the animal's eyes and surprisingly the animal waved back. David turned round to his parents but they were too busy looking at each other to notice. David then waved with two arms and again the animal copied him. David laughed and again the animal copied and laughed back strangely. David felt he had a connection with

the animal and wanted to carry on his experiment
so blew a raspberry. The animal looked a little con-
fused so David repeated it and this time the animal
responded with his own raspberry. This game was
fun thought David, but he was then interrupted by
a bell. Feeding time, David loved feeding time and
jumped up and down with excitement. The Keeper
entered the cage in the corner and threw a large
bunch of Bananas into the centre of the cage. David
bounded towards the food swung on a tree and
was munching away happily within seconds. The
animal that had been copying him was now waving
again but David was enjoying his bananas too much
to care. The animal turned to his mother and father
and made a noise.

The female reached into her bag and pulled out a ba-
nana. David saw what was happening on the other
side of the cage and laughed again.

GARDENERS
QUESTIONING TIME

Chris Barner was a very good gardener, he was also a mediocre thief who in between pruning, mowing, and cutting, used to nip through people's back doors and help himself to cash, small expensive items like phones, laptops, jewellery, etc. It was the perfect cover, travelling around the town in a van hiding as they say in plain sight. After another day's hard graft and a couple of extra burglaries, Chris Barner returned home to his modest two-bedroom bungalow plonked his bag of swag on the table and thought he'd have a few beers first and then give Carl a ring and tell him what he had to sell.

Cluso his dog ran from his basket carrying his lead and dropped it at his master's feet then gave an expectant bark.

"Go away you damn dog." He yelled, as he waved his arms about sending the dog scurrying away to safety.

"Can't I drink a beer in peace any-more?"

Chris Barner had won the dog and a parrot who never shut up talking in a game of poker down the pub a few weeks ago.

He'd intended to sell them as soon as he had got a minute but as business was doing so well and he was on a nice little earner he had just not got round to placing an ad in the corner shop window.

"WATER, WATER," The parrot suddenly burst out "WATER, WATER."

Chris Barner looked towards the cage and noted that the parrot's water bottle was empty, however ignoring it he tipped out the contents of his swag bag on the table and popped open another beer.

Several minutes later Chris Barner rang his partner in crime Carl.

Cluso feeling he was being ignored wandered out of his basket and started sniffing the swag bag that had fallen onto the floor. "Get lost mutt, no not you Carl, the damn dog is being a pest, you don't want to buy him or know someone who wants a dog do you?"

"Just the laptop, phones, and rings Chris," Carl replied.

"WATER, WATER." The parrot chirped up again.

"Hold on mate." And Chris Barner threw a blanket over the cage and told the bird to shut up one more time.

"When can you collect the stuff ?" Chris continued.

"Not until next Friday, you ok to keep hold of it till then?"

"Sure, I will hide it in the usual place no one would ever know."

Chris Barner never walked Cluso or gave the parrot any water but decided to go to the pub and spend some of his ill-gotten gains instead

Please sit down Mrs. Pemberton the inspector said as he gestured towards the chair. Please tell me everything. Mrs. Pemberton then ran through her story of how her mobile phone and rings from her bedroom had gone missing this morning and after ringing her friend Sue on the landline she learned that a couple of other neighbours had also had items go missing from their houses.

"There appears to be a well organised person or persons operating in the area and I can assure you Mrs. Pemberton we take this kind of activity very seriously and will do our best to catch the culprits.

It was not long before a keen rookie policewoman eager to impress, who had been walking the streets of the targeted neighbourhood decided to do a check on a vehicle that had been seen around the time of the robberies.

"Chris Barner, 22 Eves Close", came back the operator's voice "Has previous for burglary
, maybe drop by and have a friendly chat. "

Chris Barner was surprised when he opened the door to see the young policewoman but as cocky as ever said "Come in officer, Tea ?" Cluso who had not been out for a while took the opportunity and bolted out of the door for a much-needed pee.

"Damn dog." Barner said

The policewoman accepted the offer of a cup of tea and explained the reason for her visit.

"Mr. Barner, there have been several burglaries in the area, and as you travel about I was wondering have you seen anything suspicious lately?"

Chris Barner's mood changed "Cut to the chase Mrs. Policewoman, you think I nicked them laptops and phones don't you, well I have gone straight and have a respectable business now so sling your hook."

"Who said anything about laptops and phones ?" The policewoman said.

"LAPTOPS, PHONES AND RINGS !" the parrot shouted

"Shut it !" Chris shouted back

"LAPTOPS, PHONES, AND RINGS! " The parrot repeated

"You got a warrant ?" Chris Barner asked the policewoman

The policewoman shook her head confirming she didn't.

"The answer is no, so leave now." Chris Barner now agitated spat out

As the policewoman left the bungalow she saw the dog that had escaped out of the door digging frantically in the garden.

What you found there old boy the policewoman jokingly asked the dog.

Moving closer the policewoman could see the dog tugging at what appeared to be a sack, so decided to help the animal retrieve the item.

Much to the officer's surprise the bag contained laptops, phones, jewellery, and other items all wrapped in polythene.

"PC 4095 to control over."

"Go ahead PC 4095," Control replied

"You'll never guess what Chris Barner is growing in his garden".

Sea View

"Sign and date here please."
The registration paperwork was slid across the counter towards me and a rather worse for wear chewed Biro accompanied it. I carefully autographed the form as requested and dated 2.4.11. I smiled as I returned the paperwork and confidently asked if my request for a sea view had been received. "Just let me check." The booking in man replied. He was a small chap but judging by the size of his biceps he obviously worked out. "You're in luck, we have one left." He paused and gave me a kind smile in return.

"I hope your stay will be an enjoyable one, if you follow me I will show you to your room." We went along several corridors and then up a couple of flights of stairs before he suddenly stopped outside number 21. "Oh! what a coincidence 21 my lucky number." I stepped inside and took a brief look around as the door was shut hard behind me. 21 I chuckled, the number of years that I will spend in this cell. I walked to the small barred window and stood on my tiptoes. "The lying sod! You can't see the sea from here."

The final story is an adventure about Bert and Maureen. I intend to publish a book in 2022 following the retired couple over 12 months Starting with January,
Chapter one will be A new years revolution. Maureen has singed them both up at the local gym in order to trim back waistlines following Christmas over indulgences.
Bert is not happy at all and tries every trick possible to avoid the treadmill.

This sample chapter is mid year and features the month of May.
It's a Readers Digest version of 50 shades meets B and Q.

THE ADVENTURES OF BERT AND MAUREEN

21 sheds in May

"One crumpet or two?"

"Two please and make them crispy."Bert replied glancing up from his paper

"If I don't know how you like your crumpets after 25 years of marriage then I never will." Maureen whispered under her breath.

Bert never heard her as he was tutting and shaking his head at the latest opinion polls, that claimed both parties were ahead in the election race and that another MP had defected to The Twiddling Thumbs Party.

"They are all as bad as each other."Bert barked "Out for themselves and sod everyone else."

"Yes dear." Maureen mumbled

But Bert's sudden outburst faded as he reminded himself he had a great Bank holiday Monday planned. The sun was already high in the sky and the temperature was a pleasant 22C, not a cloud in sight and for once, the British Bank Holiday Monday was not a washout. Bert's agenda for the day comprised of

9.30-10.30am mow lawn (Look busy)

10.30-11.00am analyze football fixtures with a cup of coffee and three cheeky chocolate biscuits behind the garden shed out of site of Maureen

11.00-12 noon have a walk to the bookies via Alfs and get his orbital sander back he had lent him. Not that Bert intended to do any sanding either orbital or up and down sanding, but he felt Alf had had his sander for far too long and he did not want Alf to think he didn't want it back.

12 noon -1pm lunch in the garden with Maureen (mention what a good job of mowing he had done)

1pm – 2pm light snooze, in the garden

2pm – 5pm afternoon beverage of the San Miguel type accompanied by several more of the same

5pm – 6pm walk to bookies to collect winnings via The Old Grey Horse pub or if unlucky just to the pub and sample the ambiance of the beer garden

6pm – 7pm evening meal with Maureen

7pm – 8pm free time

8pm- 10pm Soaps catch up or watch a film. Maureen had hinted she wanted to watch some romantic chick flick as they were now known, but hey Bert thought if it will keep her happy he can go with it

,

Maureen sat down next to Bert and waited until he caught her eye.

"Bert! today we are going to get a new shed, I have been doing some research and made a list of all the companies within a 10-mile radius that are open today. We are leaving at 9.30am."

Bert's plans evaporated within a split second. No relaxing, no walk to the bookies, no San Miguel, no Old Grey Horse, no point in trying to talk her out of it.

Dreams shattered, Bert put down his paper and was about to speak when he could feel her eyes burning into his skin waiting for a response.

"I'll get my shoes." and Bert did. Bert was convinced that the gods must be conspiring against him as it was a rare occasion when the weather was so lovely and he had the opportunity to "Kickback" as his nephew often said. At 9.30am on the dot, Bert and Maureen left the driveway in their Mondeo, windows down and the radio tuned into smooth FM. Bill Withers telling everyone it was a "Lovely day, Lovely day, Lovely day,...... Lovely day". Was Bill Withers looking for a shed Bert thought, obviously not as he wouldn't be singing that? "Did you bring the tape measure, Bert ?" Maureen asked   "Er, No I forgot." Bert replied hiding a grin

"Well, it's a good job I brought it then." Bert's first attempt at sabotage proved futile. As they arrived at sheds2go Bert noticed a few more couples looking around already. He also noticed that the majority were glum-looking blokes trailing behind their wives or partners no doubt also pining for their lost day of relaxation. Several sheds later Bert's enthusiasm increased as he realized that the shed they would buy would be his sanctuary and that he needed to have an input as he intended to have a tv, radio, and a comfy chair placed in there so it had to be big enough. Bert stepped into another shed and tried to imagine himself sitting in his chair looking out of the door with the Tv in the corner and a small table for his brew. The window wasn't big enough on this one and the door opened the wrong way. Four hours later Bert pulled into another car park of a company selling sheds but he soon perked up when he noticed that this one was also a small garden centre that had a café. "Maureen, can I treat you to a coffee and perhaps a cake?" Maureen who only had to hear the word cake and was put into an instant state of instant happiness looked fondly at Bert and said "Go on then Bert, why not, it is Bank Holiday."Bert who had seen the café sign, however, failed to see the bank holiday opening times which later would prove costly. The coffee was very well deserved and the cake did hardly touch Maureen's lips as it disappeared quicker than Usain Bolt in his world record 100m sprint. "Bert, shall we push the boat out and go to the Old Grey Horse for tea, we can drop the car off first and then have a walk ?" Bert also perked up instantly and said. "That would be nice love." "You've not called me love for ages," Maureen replied. The odds of him having a few pints increased dramatically and he felt a new lease of energy. "I will just nip to the little boys room and then let's see what they have here, I saw a shed on the way in that looked about the right size and had a double window." Now some people would call it fate, some would call it karma but Maureen and Bert stepped into the shed Bert had seen from the car park and it looked perfect. "The spec said it is made from the finest Canadian timbcr and has double glazing, double glazing, can you believe it". Bert enthusiastically read. "It also has one of the most secure locking mechanisms for sheds on the market". Bert added ,Bert swung the door shut and it clicked. "Even the click screams quality, forged iron from Sheffield". Bert continued to tap and examine every part of the shed. Once they were both happy that this was the shed for them, they decided on a strategy to get a bit knocked off the price. "If we start with £100.00 off and try from there" Bert proclaimed. Bert went to the door and tried to pull it open, but it didn't budge. He pulled again and tried turning the handle backward and forwards but still it didn't open. Maureen stepped up to the door "Let me have a go" and tried several more times to open the door. Bert by this time had moved over to the window, but it had a key locking mechanism on it and the key was nowhere to be seen. Bert tapped on the window in the hope of attracting someone's attention. He pressed his cheek against the pain and looked as far to the left and right of the shed as he could, but he still could not see anyone. "Help ! here, anyone". Bert shouted at the top of his voice "Bert, get a grip". Maureen shouted over the top of Bert. "Someone will come by soon and see or hear us and let us out, there's no need to get hysterical". But that was not going to happen. The staff were keen to leave and enjoy what was left of the bank holiday. Barbecues to attend, sunbathing perhaps and so as soon as the hand struck 3pm the office was shut down, lights off and the gates secured, their car wheels leaving a cloud of dust, which soon settled and then all was still. "What time do they shut"? Maureen asked Bert "Probably 4pm, so that gives us an hour as it has just passed 3pm "Try ringing the garden centre". Maureen suddenly said "My phones in the car". "How many times have I told you not to leave your phone in the car" Maureen added "Surely they will see our car in the car park" Bert and Maureen were sat on the floor of the shed both wondering what they could do. The gods were definitely conspiring against Bert and his chances of a pint or two in the Old Grey Horse now seemed very unlikely. "Shall we play eye spy" Maureen suggested "Eye spy, eye bloody spy, there's nothing in here except you me and air, what is there to bloody spy" "Ok, ok just an idea to pass the time". Maureen quickly replied Bert then said "Eye spy with my little eye something beginning with B" Maureen then spent a couple of minutes trying to guess. As nothing began with B except Bert, Maureen gave up. "Do you give up"? Bert smugly said "Yes, I give up what begins with B". "Beauty" Bert proudly pronounced

"Beauty, what's beauty"? Maureen quizzically asked "You are," Bert said as he gently put his arm around her and kissed her fondly on the lips. "Oh Bert what has come over you" Maureen kissed him back and soon they were both holding each other tightly as Bert whispered sweet nothings into Maureen's ear. The next 15 minutes were a bit of a blur to Maureen and Bert as they pulled at each other's clothes Although Bert did still having the presence of mind to tuck his socks into his shoes, they explored each other's bodies just like they had done in 1974 in the dunes, on a day trip to Lytham St Anne's. The windows of the shed now fully steamed up, the problem of them being trapped inside a long distant memory. Bert and Maureen lay motionless on the floor of the shed completely exhausted. They were dripping in sweat. Clothes were strewn all over except for Bert's socks and shoes in the corner. "I love you, Maureen," Bert said "you are a beauty and always will be" "I love you to Bert" Maureen replied "You just needed to know it" They dressed and tried to make themselves look half decent and not look like two teenagers that had been fooling around in a shed.

Maureen then very discreetly removed the key to the shed door from her pocket and unlocked the door without Bert seeing.

"Have another go at the lock Bert" Maureen suggested.

Bert fiddled with the door and then to his surprise it swung open.

"I've done it Maureen" Bert shouted

"Well done Bert, now let's get to the Old Grey Horse, I'm gasping".

Bert did not need asking twice.

"Shall we ring and book a table Maureen". Bert asked

"We better had with it being a bank holiday" Maureen agreed

Bert pulled out his phone from his trouser pocket

"I thought you had left your phone in the car."Maureen said

Bert winked.

"What a glorious bank holiday."

to be continued.....

Twenty two short tales with a twist is due for release in 2023

Printed in Great Britain
by Amazon